Bobby Normal
And The
Eternal Talisman

A.S.Chambers

To Pam
Lovely to see you again
Austin :)

DEDICATION

For children the world over.
May your life be one big adventure.

ALSO BY A.S.CHAMBERS:

Sam Spallucci Series.
The Casebook of Sam Spallucci - 2012
Sam Spallucci: Ghosts From The Past - 2014
Sam Spallucci: Shadows of Lancaster – 2016
Sam Spallucci: The Case of The Belligerent Bard - 2016
Sam Spallucci: Dark Justice – 2018
Sam Spallucci: Troubled Souls - 2020
Sam Spallucci: Bloodline – Due 2021
Sam Spallucci: Fury of the Fallen - Due 2022

Short Story Anthologies.
Oh Taste And See – 2014
All Things Dark And Dangerous – 2015
Let All Mortal Flesh – 2016
Mourning Has Broken – 2018
Hide Not Thou Thy Face - 2020
If Ye Loathe Me – Due 2022

Ebook short stories.
High Moon - 2013
Girls Just Wanna Have Fun – 2013
Needs Must - 2019

Novellas.
Songbird – 2019

Bobby Normal Series.
Bobby Normal and the Virtuous Man - Due 2022

Omnibuses.
Children of Cain - 2019

ACKNOWLEDGEMENTS

A huge thank you to the lovely Theresa Hughes for her, as
always, excellent proofreading skills.
Plus many, many thanks to the incredibly talented Liam
Shaw for once more putting up with my incredibly vague
ideas and producing yet another magnificent cover.

CONTENTS

Chapter One   1

Chapter Two   13

Chapter Three   25

Chapter Four   43

Chapter Five   53

Chapter Six   63

Chapter Seven   73

Chapter Eight   83

Author's Notes   99

Chapter One

People called this place the Divergent Lands. It was a world where there was poor sanitation, little food and monsters lurked around every corner. You could see your loved ones drive their wagon to market in the morning, only to have the same cart carry their cold, stiff corpse home the following evening.

To Bobby it was home.

Sure, it was far from perfect. There were everyday problems to encounter: be quick with your fingers; be careful who you annoy; know when to scarper and always remember to tolerate your kid sister.

Right now, the fourth of these was causing Bobby the most trouble.

"But I don't want to get up!" whined the pile of filthy rags in the corner of the abandoned hut that the two children currently called their home.

"You know we have to get going. Teller saw us last night. He'll know we're here and he'll be after us. You really want that?"

The jumble of rags uttered a far from pleasant noise. "I'm asleep," they said, then proceeded to snore loudly.

Bobby grabbed the dirty bedding and snatched it back. His kid sister glowered up at him, her chestnut brown eyes shining up from her grimy face.

"Not fair."

"Come on Katy," Bobby pleaded desperately. "You know what happened the last time he caught us."

The little eight-year-old gave one more huff and surrendered, albeit ungraciously, rolling her eyes as she sat up. She wriggled out of her mess of a bed before running her fingers through the straggles of knots that made up her hair. "I'm hungry."

"Well we'd better do something about that," Bobby grinned.

It was market day, which meant that there was plenty of food to fill a hungry teenage boy and his young sister. Not that they intended to *trade* for any. It wasn't as if they had anything of value with which they could barter. They were just worthless street urchins.

They had been since the day that their father had died.

Katy was too young to remember either of their parents and Bobby possessed just the vaguest memories of their mother, but not a day went past that Bobby had to hide a tear as he recalled the strength of their love. One day, when Katy had just been a little babe in arms, his dad had taken them to market to get some provisions. He had been a woodworker, so there was always a demand for his creations: stools, tables, other items of furniture. This meant that, when they were young, they had never felt the twisted bite of hunger in their bellies. On that day, when he was exchanging a fine willow basket for some vegetables, his dad had turned to Bobby and said, "You know, it wasn't always like this. Back hundreds of years ago, people used to have to pay for things." He had smiled at Bobby's confused face. "They had shiny pieces of metal that they exchanged for goods. People called them coins. No use for them these days. Not since *they* came."

Bobby remembered that conversation as if it were yesterday.

He had good reason to.

It was at that moment that he had seen his first construct.

It had been taller than the average man, broader across the chest. It walked on two legs and a pair of arms swayed rhythmically by its side. But that was where any similarities ended. This was no creature of flesh and blood. Its skin, if that's what it was, was the colour and sheen of mud from the nearby river. It rippled and undulated as the beast strode unhindered through the marketplace. People stood in silence as it passed. Mothers shielded their children from its gaze.

Not that it had any eyes, nor a neck.

The construct's chest seemed to rise

up into what it possessed for a head, rounding off at the top. Across the middle of the face was a jagged slit that opened and shut, causing its skin to part and its deformed tongue to slither as its breathing rasped noisily.

It was the obscenest thing that Bobby had ever lain eyes upon, yet he had stood and stared up at the giant whilst others had cowered in fear.

"Bobby," his father had whispered. "Look away, lad."

But he had not. He had seen the monster and it could never be unseen.

The creature had paused in front of him and his father. It had turned and bent low, its face level with his. There had been startled cries from the other villagers and he had felt his father's fingers like a vice on his shoulder.

But Bobby did not flinch. He just stood and stared up at the monstrosity.

Then a curious sound gurgled from the belly of the beast, as if rocks were being rolled around inside an old wooden barrel. And Bobby realised that the construct was laughing at him. The noise ebbed away as the monster drew itself up. It turned and continued its solitary march out of town.

As one, the whole market resumed its breath. Bobby felt himself swept up into his father's arms and embraced in a hug that could have crushed an oak tree.

In the here and now, he smoothed a stray tear into the side of his face. "What do we want to eat today?" he asked his sister.

"Apples!" she shouted with glee.

Bobby grinned. It was always apples. "Well, you know what you have to do then."

"Oh my! What is it little one?" The elderly man stooped to inspect the small girl that was sat sobbing in the middle of the muddy road. "You'll get trodden on if you stay there."

"I've lost my mummy," Katy whimpered, rubbing the heel of her hand at the most realistic tears of woe that a child could possibly manufacture. "Have you seen her?"

The old man frowned as he peered around the busy market square. He removed his threadbare cap and scratched at his thinning scalp with chipped fingernails. "I don't know. What does she look like?"

"My mummy," Katy volunteered not-very-helpfully.

The man frowned. "Look, you can't stay there. Why don't I help you get up off the road?" He bent to take her by the arm.

Then the screaming began.

Immediately, concerned heads turned in their direction.

The man froze in panic. "What? What's the matter?"

Still the child screamed.

"Here, what you doing to the kiddie?" demanded a rather large woman with ruddy cheeks and a somewhat grating voice.

"Well, nothing," the poor man protested.

"Then why's she screaming?"

Katy cracked open an eye and peered up at her elderly helper then proceeded to crank the volume up even further.

"What's going on?" came another voice.

"This old man's hurt this little one."

"Well, I never."

"But I only asked her what was wrong."

"Some people…"

From the corner of the square, Bobby carefully crept behind the mass of people fighting to see what was causing such a fuss. When he was sure that no one was looking, he swept handfuls of fruit into his tunic. When it was full to overflowing, he stuck two fingers in his mouth and blew a sharp whistle that rose above the hubbub. From between the legs of the mob baying for the blood of the unfortunate Good Samaritan, Katy crawled on her hands and knees.

"Come on," Bobby whispered. "Time to go."

It almost went without a hitch.

Almost.

"Hey!"

Bobby turned and saw a group of older boys running towards them, across the market square.

"Teller," he moaned. "Quick, Katy. Run!"

So they did.

The feet of the two youngsters squelched and splattered through the muddy streets. They didn't dare look back for fear of losing ground. Not that they needed to check if they were still being pursued; the sound of Teller and his gang of thugs echoed through the empty alleyways, informing the young thieves as to exactly where the older boys were.

After a short while, Bobby could feel his lungs start to burn and he could see through the tears of exertion in his eyes that Katy was also fit to drop. "Quick! Down here!" He yanked his little sister through a series of small alleys until they reached a shadowed courtyard. "If we're lucky, they might run past."

However, luck had decided not to favour them that day.

"They went this way!"

The older boys turned the corner and stood across the entrance to the dead end. Bobby and Katy were trapped. Teller swaggered up in front of his three cronies, his wicked smile looking even more vile in the gloom of the side street. "Nowhere to hide, *Normal*," he leered.

"Don't call me that," Bobby managed through gasps of hot air as he tried to regain his breath.

"I'll call you what I want, street trash," Teller spat, his chest puffed up like a sail on a barge that has caught a strong tailwind. "You're *normal* and there's nothing you can do about it. Now come here and get the thrashing you deserve." He reached into his belt and drew out the evil-looking whip that he always carried on his person.

Bobby pushed Katy protectively behind him as he frantically looked around them for a means of escape. There were a few old boxes and some battered barrels by a wall, but they were both exhausted and, by the time they had started to climb, Teller and his cronies would be upon them.

He felt the purloined apples in his tunic jiggle about against his chest. He pulled one out and held it up threateningly.

A harsh bray of confident laughter burst from Teller's narrow lips. "Seriously? You're gonna defend yourself with a piece of fruit?" Shaking his head, he drew his whip hand back. Bobby did likewise with the apple.

Just as the older boy was about to let the whip fly and inflict serious harm on Bobby, there was a twanging noise and the bully crumpled down onto one knee, dropping his whip and clutching at his temple that was now miraculously oozing blood. He shouted out in equal amounts of surprise and pain.

"Up here! Now!" came another voice, a female one this time, from behind them.

Bobby spun around and saw a figure atop the wall by the boxes and barrels. He did not need telling twice. He hefted Katy onto the pile of wooden packaging and helped her scramble upwards. He clambered up in her wake as another twang rang out from above, closely followed by a second scream of agony from down below.

"In there." Their saviour motioned to an open window, its shutters rotten and fallen away. "Run through the building. I'll follow."

They did as they were directed and emerged on a neighbouring street.

Their companion joined them and Bobby saw their face for the first time, surrounded by a brown hood, trimmed with purple. It was a girl, not much older than him. She winked and stowed a small cata-pult away in her belt. "Let's keep walking," she instructed and guided them away from the building.

Away from the alley.

Away from Teller.

Chapter Two

A short while later, Bobby and Katy were warming themselves in front of an impromptu fire in one of the many abandoned buildings of Irlingbury as they and their new friend tucked into their well-earned haul of juicy apples.

"What did you say your name was again?" Katy mumbled around a mouthful of half-chewed fruit, watery juice dribbling down her chin.

The other girl smiled. "Persephone," she replied for the third time.

The youngster frowned. "Funny name," she said.

"Katy!" her brother scolded. "Don't be rude. Especially after she saved us from Teller."

The youngster gave a sigh that demonstrated just how often she suffered her older sibling's despair. "Sorrrrrryyyy…" she apologised half-heartedly.

"That's okay," the redheaded girl smiled. "It *is* an unusual name for these parts."

"You're not from round here then?" Bobby asked, curiosity getting the better of him. Normally, his and Katy's existence was a simple one of feeling hungry, stealing food and being chased until they either escaped or were caught and punished. Now, this newcomer had burst into their lives, altering that mundane balance, and he just had to know more about her.

Persephone shook her head. "No. Just passing through, really."

Bobby gave a small laugh.

"What is it?"

"No one ever comes to Irlingbury. We never see travellers."

The girl looked sad. "*Nowhere* sees travellers these days, Bobby. It's not safe."

"But *you're* travelling," he pointed out.

"I'm supposed to deliver something."

14

She absentmindedly poked at the fire with a charred stick, causing small embers to spit and the flames to jump around like living creatures. "Why were those older boys chasing you?"

"Because they smell!" Katy piped up.

Bobby rolled his eyes. *Sisters.*

Persephone giggled. "I'm sure they do."

"It's actually because we're orphans," Bobby explained. "Teller and his gang come from whole families, which is so rare these days. They see themselves as better than everybody else."

"That's awful. Is that why they called you *Normal*? Because they see themselves as special? Privileged?"

Bobby nodded. "They see us as beneath them. They are the high and mighty ones. We are just oxen to be whipped into pulling their carts and do the jobs that they find undesirable. Nothing special. Normal."

"One of these days," Katy grumbled, "I'll show Teller what's for."

Bobby rolled his eyes once more at her eight-year-old ire.

Persephone frowned. "It strikes me that they have a very skewed view on life, but then that's not surprising these days. The things I have seen on my travels…" She drifted off momentarily before focussing once more on the fire. "To me, being normal seems like a wonderful thing. What I wouldn't give to have a touch of normality in my life right now." Then, without the slightest warning, she started to cry.

Katy opened her mouth in shock and the piece of apple she had been eating plopped out into her lap. Bobby crossed the room and lay a hand on the older girl's shoulder. "Are… are you okay?"

Persephone sat up, rubbed the heel of her hand into her eye and pulled herself together. "I'm sorry. It's just that… Oh, I can't pull you into this. It's not fair on you."

"I'm sure it's not *that* bad," Bobby said reassuringly.

Persephone gave a deep sigh, looked him square in the face and said, "Actually, the fate of the world might depend upon it."

For a moment, Bobby was fearfully

quiet. Here was a girl that he and his sister had only just met. True, she had saved their skins from Teller and his thugs but to be told that they were being drawn into fate of the world stuff…

Eventually, he said, "Well, we owe you. So, whatever it is, I guess we're in."

"Really?"

"It's not like we've got anything else to do," he shrugged.

Katy just sat oblivious, munching on another apple.

Persephone reached into a faded leather pouch which was attached to her corded belt and pulled out a small wooden token. "This," she explained, "is the Eternal Talisman." She passed it over for Bobby to take a look at. It was about the size of the palm of his hand and on one side was a burnt etching of what looked like a fancy cup and a sword.

"What's it for?" the boy asked, turning the artefact over in his hands. "It doesn't look very special."

"It needs to reach a man in the next village, Orchester," Persephone continued.

"For the likes of you or me, it has no use, but for him…" She trailed off and Bobby saw tears start to form in her eyes once again.

"What will he use it for?"

"It will help him kill Kanor."

Bobby's eyes widened to the size of dinner plates. "You know *Kanor*?" His voice was no more than a whisper, as if even the walls around him were not supposed to hear the name.

Persephone shook her head. "No. I don't. No one does. You know that. You also know what that monster has done to our land. The dragon has ravaged it, burnt it to a husk and trampled upon those that remain. It wasn't always like this, you know, Bobby? Once, there were fields as far as the eye could see where people grew an abundance of crops. There were majestic cities with buildings that rose into the sky.

"And even the sky was not the limit," she continued. "People fashioned powerful craft that could take us away from here, out into the darkest of nights to visit other planets and far off places.

"Then the Divergence came and Kanor

stole this world from us overnight. He devoured our dreams like a hungry monster that had been lurking under our bed; biding its time, waiting for the right moment to strike."

Bobby sat and listened quietly. His father had told him tales of times long, long ago. Tales that echoed what Persephone had just described. Bobby had just discounted them as funny bedtime tales; men flying through the air, buildings the colour of which could be changed at the touch of a button. These were surely just things of fancy? Things with which to entertain a five-year-old boy as he was tucked into bed at night.

Or perhaps they were real?

"The constructs are his creations, aren't they?" Bobby asked, already knowing it to be the truth. "They're not of the natural order."

"That's right. He fashioned them from clay and sent them across the globe in the shape of normal human beings. They dwelt amongst us for thousands of years. We were unaware of their existence. We never knew that they lived next door to us and laboured with us at our places of work.

"That was how they were able to slaughter almost everyone in one single, crushing blow.

"When the Divergence came, Kanor rose and called out to his children. They took their true form and butchered without mercy all those that they saw until humanity was reduced to a pitiful remnant. Now all we are good for is to provide sport for Kanor and those that have thrown their lot in with him.

"He has to be stopped."

Katy finished munching on her stolen fruit. "Why can't you take that thing to Orchester?"

Sadness clouded the older girl's face. "My father is sick. Very sick. I have received word that he has but a few days left. I have my duty to deliver the Talisman, but the need to see my father before he dies is calling to me in a louder voice. I fear that I will not make it back in time."

Bobby looked at Katy. She shrugged.

"We'll do it," he said. "What is the name of the man that we should find?"

"His name is Jason." Persephone lay the Eternal Talisman in Bobby's palm and gripped his hand tight. "You must not let anyone know about this. No one at all. Kanor has spies everywhere. Remember that. Also remember that constructs can change shape. They may not all look like the abominations we see around from time to time. They can look just like you or me…

"Until it's too late."

They stayed there that night: Bobby, Katy and Persephone. Katy drifted off to sleep within minutes and the older girl was not far behind. Bobby, however, found it much harder to switch off. His life had been changed in an instant. This morning, it had all been about simply surviving and finding the next meal whilst avoiding bullies like Teller. Now, it was the fate of the world and the powerful monster known only as Kanor.

He tossed and turned next to the fire, trying to achieve some level of comfort. When he did finally nod off, the few hours he grabbed were filled with dreams of being chased, not by Teller, but by staggering con-

21

structs, their clay-like arms reaching out to grab at him.

In his dreams, he ran out of the city onto a great plain of grass. In front of him lay a huge lake that stretched a great distance. In its midst was an island and, on that, an old building with a spire that reached up to the heavens. He had to reach the building, he knew he must, but how could he cross the lake?

Then the constructs were upon him. He heard them shuffling up behind him and he ran for the lake but, as he did so, the sound of cruel laughter drifting across the water from the island reached his ears and overhead, above the ruined building, an immense obsidian shadow spread its vast wings and rose into the sky.

Bobby woke with a start. His heart was pounding and his mouth was dry. Persephone was already awake and frowned at him. "You okay?" she asked. "You were dreaming."

Bobby shook his head violently from side to side. He wanted rid of that image of the dark shadow. It did not belong inside of him.

"I'm okay," he reassured her. "When are we leaving?"

"As soon as your sister wakes up."

Bobby glanced over at Katy who was snoring loudly. "I'd better wake her then, or we'll be here all day."

A.S.Chambers

Chapter Three

"So how will we know where to find this man called Jason?"

The three youths were approaching the edge of the village. The buildings were even more dilapidated out here. Once, it had been a thriving suburb where proud parents had happily watched their beloved and cherished children play in neat, well-tended gardens; now it was just a haunt for thieves and beggars who would grab you from the shadows, slit your throat and make off with the rags on your back. It was a perfect symbol of what the land had become post-Divergence.

Persephone pondered the question. "I was told that there is a small house on what is left of the main road into the village. It bears a white door upon which there is a green mark, a face of some kind. You need to knock there and say that you have come to deliver the goods. Those inside will know what to do."

Bobby frowned. It all sounded very vague, not to mention dangerous. He cast his eyes back down the street along which they had walked. True, Irlingbury was not much, but at least he knew it like the back of his hand. He had never left its borders before; the world outside was a strange and unfamiliar place.

Persephone could clearly see the hesitation in his face. "If… If you don't want to do this, I'll understand."

Bobby sighed. How could he refuse? The sadness in her voice was heart-breaking. She had a sick father to whom she desperately needed to return. *His* father was dead. How would he feel if he had just one final chance to say goodbye? It was right that he and Katy do this for her.

"No," he said. "I'm okay. We'll be fine."

He felt an insistent tug on his sleeve. Looking down he saw a concerned look on

Katy's face. "I'm not so sure we will be." She pointed down the road that led out of the village and Bobby groaned.

Teller and his gang were stood on the perimeter of the village.

"I thought we'd lost them," he groaned. As he whipped his head to and fro, looking desperately for a place to hide, he heard an excited shout go up from the older boys. "Quick!" Bobby said, darting into the ruins of the dilapidated buildings. "This way."

The three companions ran away from the main road and started to jink left and right through the run-down suburbs. All the while they were aware of the clattering of footsteps and whoops of excitement from Teller and his crew. The tumble-down housing was a rabbit warren, with holes and rubble to dart behind and hide underneath, but the thugs were persistent and it was soon apparent that they were not going to lose them easily.

"What are we going to do?" Persephone whispered in an agitated voice as they caught their breath in the remains of a small house. "We need to get out of here."

Bobby shook his head. "I know. I know. I just don't know how we can shake them."

"What about the tunnels?"

Bobby turned to his sister. "That's an excellent idea!"

"Tunnels?" Persephone asked. "What tunnels?"

"There are tunnels under the village," Bobby explained. "Dad told us that their old job was to take waste water and other stuff..."

"Poop!" chipped in Katy.

"Yeah, poop," Bobby continued. "They used to take all that stuff away from the village. Sometimes, when we have nowhere else to go, we hide down there because Teller and his crew won't go down there. They see themselves better than that. It's not pleasant, but it does from time to time. The best thing is that the tunnels lead out of the village. They should get us past Teller."

"How do we get into them?"

Bobby cautiously craned his neck around the rotten doorframe of the old house. "I can see a way in just up the street. It's a metal plate in the road." Then he frowned. As he looked down the street, he was sure that he had seen something, or was it some*one*, moving in the shadows of another rundown house. Then he snapped back into his hiding place as he heard the sound of running coming in the other direction.

"But we've got to get to it without being seen," he grumbled.

Then the most curious thing happened.

A shout went up in the street. "There he is! There's Normal." At first Bobby felt chilled to the bone. He had been spotted and Teller was going to capture them, but then the sound of running clattered past and he heard a voice call out, "There he goes! Around that corner!"

The three listened to the sound of Teller and the others running away from their hiding place.

"We'd better go," Persephone insisted and crawled out from the ruined house. Bobby and Katy followed. She pointed to a round metal object in the surface of the road. "Is that the way into the tunnels?"

Bobby ran up to the disc and slid his

fingers into an eroded gap at the side. He heaved and lifted its covering up. The three of them peered down into an uncertain gloom. "We'd better hurry," he said. "I don't know who Teller's chasing, but when he finds out it's not me, he'll be back.

"And he won't be happy."

One by one, the three companions climbed down a rusted metal ladder that was vaguely fastened to the side of the access hole. Bobby was the last one to descend and, as he did, he slid the cover back into place, plunging them into complete darkness.

There was a flash of sparks and he blinked as a fire blossomed in front of them. Persephone had pulled a small torch out of her backpack and had ignited the cloth around the end. "I hope this passage isn't too long," she frowned over the flickering source of light. "There's not too much life in this. I just keep it for emergencies."

Bobby looked off into the all-encompassing gloom. "It's not far. The tunnel will run down the main road then out of Irlingbury." He pointed off into the darkness. "We just need to head that way to reach the main tunnel then turn right and keep going."

"Just look out for rats," chipped in his kid sister. "They're really big and they bite."

The children edged their way cautiously along the side tunnel, the glow from Persephone's torch doing an adequate job of highlighting any obstacles that lay in their way. "You say these are left over from long ago?" the older girl asked as she picked her way over a fallen stone.

Bobby nodded. "Dad said that they were built before the Divergence, before society fell to bits."

They sidled around a hole in the floor of the tunnel. Bobby tried not to think about what creatures might be lurking down there; creatures that could see a lot better in the dark than he could.

"There's so much that we lost," Persephone said. "So much knowledge, so much society. It has to be put right."

"You think that this man called Jason will be able to do that?"

She nodded, vehemently. "He has to.

He is special. He's the Virtuous Man." She turned and saw the look of incomprehension on Bobby's face, so explained: "There is a prophecy, from before the Divergence. *'He who rose like a dragon of old will be slain by the man of virtue.'* You see what that means? Jason is the one who will free us. He will slay Kanor."

Bobby frowned. "How can one man slay a dragon? Surely, he won't be a match?"

The tiniest of smiles on Persephone's lips was illuminated by her flickering torch. "First, Kanor isn't *really* a dragon. Those things have never existed. They were myths and legends from millennia ago. He is just a man, a powerful one albeit, but just a man. He's referred to as a dragon because of the fear that he strikes in our hearts. Second, Jason *will* be victorious because that is exactly what he does not feel: fear. He is full of virtue and lives his life for the sole purpose of freeing us from this tyranny."

Bobby shrugged. He remained unconvinced. "If you say so, I guess. But it all just sounds like words to me."

"Well, don't forget that it's not just the prophecy. There's the talisman too. If the talisman exists, then the prophecy must surely be true."

Bobby saw the logic in what she said. Words were, well, just words. Anyone could make them up and spread them around. But for there to be something physical, something tangible to back them up, that made them far more real. "I suppose it gives us something to believe in, doesn't it?"

He saw Persephone nod her head above the flickering light as they reached the junction where their offshoot joined the main tunnel. They turned around the corner and paused as something caught their attention.

"What was that?" Persephone asked.

They listened and the unmistakable pattering of tiny feet rose from a faint echo to an oncoming rush.

"That'll be the rats," Katy explained, her eyes wide in the half light. "We should run now."

So they did.

As the thousands of tiny feet crescendoed into a roar, the children chased after the glowing torch, dodging as best they could the random pieces of fallen stonework and discarded detritus that lay around the main tunnel of the sewer. Every now and then, the torch would flicker as the rushing air brushed against its flame. They held their breath as it burst anew into life and guided their way along the tunnel, away from the following swarm of rats.

And what a swarm it was that was pursuing them.

Once, just once, Bobby allowed himself a hurried glance over his shoulder and wished that he hadn't. It was close to pitch black behind them but, in the glow of the torch, it was as if the floor and the walls were moving. The surface of the rock seemed to undulate in the shadows and from the midst of the pattering feet a new noise could be heard; an unmistakably hungry squeaking. He snapped his head back to the front and almost tumbled as Persephone yanked him sharply to a halt. He tottered and swayed as his arms pin wheeled and his eyes boggled at the sheer drop in front of him. Part of the floor had collapsed and he had almost plummeted into a dark void.

"We're trapped!" Katy screamed out.

Bobby frantically looked around. There had to be a way across. There had to. Then, in the glimmer of the torch he saw something lying against the wall. He ran over and grabbed it. It was an old piece of wood. He had no idea what it was doing here, but it looked like it would be their saviour. "Help me!" he called out.

Persephone and his kid sister helped him drag the plank of wood to the hole. Between the three of them, they swung it out and over the chasm, so that it sat flat on the far side.

"Quick!" Persephone bounded across the wood to the other side. "Just don't look down!"

Katy looked up at Bobby, fear in her eyes.

"Go on," he reassured her. "I'll be right behind you."

She inhaled a small courage-gathering breath, then scampered across the plank.

The noise behind Bobby was getting

even louder. He snuck a quick glance behind him and saw that the rats were almost at his ankles. He turned and bolted for the plank, but the light was poor and he hadn't judged his route as carefully as the others. Just two steps in and he felt his body lurch to one side. He was aware of Katy screaming out to him and his arms flailing around in an insane manner as he forced his feet to continue one after the other. He had to get across; he could not leave Katy on her own. Focussing his eyes on his sister, who stood beneath the glow of Persephone's torch, he levelled himself up and ran straight ahead. He ignored the bouncing of the plank beneath him and flew off the wood onto the other side, collapsing in a heap at his sister's feet.

Turning his head, he watched in horror as the rats reached the makeshift bridge. They crowded onto it and began to traverse the chasm. Persephone screamed out in a shriek of rage and heaved against the wood with all her weight. Bobby and Katy joined her and they watched as it tumbled down into the dark, taking the rats that were running along its surface with it.

The three sat for a moment catching their breath.

Finally, Katy let out a deep sigh and said, "Do you have any more of those apples? That made me rather hungry."

The ladder up to the surface was not far along from the chasm. The three of them blinked repeatedly as their eyes adjusted to the bright light of day.

"I never want to see another rat as long as I live," Persephone muttered.

Bobby and Katy nodded in agreement. They peered down the road and Irlingbury was now away in the distance.

"Well, I guess this is where we part company," the older girl said as she extinguished her torch. "Remember, you mustn't tell anyone about the Talisman and Jason is in a house with a white door on the road into Orchester. There will be a green face painted on the woodwork and you need to say that you have come to deliver the goods."

"We'll make sure that he gets it."

Persephone smiled. "Well, I wish you luck. Walk well and stay safe."

"Walk well and stay safe," Bobby and Katy replied together.

The girl turned and looked back at Irlingbury. "I'll skirt around the edge of the village. I don't want another run in with our *friends*. Thanks again," she said.

They watched as Persephone made her way back down the road before turning North when she reached the outskirts of the settlement.

"Well, it's just you and me now," Bobby said to his sister.

"It always is," she replied as they walked away in the opposite direction.

For a while, they walked in silence, the tattered buildings falling far away behind them and the barren countryside stretching out in front. Eventually, Katy piped up, "What do you think Orchester will be like?"

Bobby pondered this for a moment. He had never left Irlingbury before and had very little information about the wider world. "I'm not sure," he eventually replied. "I guess it'll be a bit like home, perhaps a bit busier."

"Why do you think it'll be busier?"

"*Anywhere* will be busier than home."

The two children laughed.

That night, the two siblings slept out in a field. The air was warm and there was no sign of rain, the black sky clear above. They hunkered down beneath a wiry hedgerow to make sure that they were unseen by any un-friendly passers-by and allowed themselves time to relax after the excitement of the day.

Bobby looked over at Katy and saw that her eyes were fixed on the full moon, high above. "What are you thinking?" he asked.

"Do you think the moon is a long way away?"

"Definitely."

"Further than Orchester?"

Bobby smiled. "Oh yes."

"What about Wellington?"

"The moon is so far away that we could never get there."

The small girl pursed her lips. "Do you think people have *ever* got to the moon?"

Bobby rolled onto his back and gazed

up at the white orb with its mysterious patterns etched into its pale face. "I don't see how. It's not as if we could fly, is it?"

"I know… But what about *before*?" The word was filled with childish awe. "Weren't people supposed to do all manner of incredible things? Persephone said that they went to other planets. Perhaps they flew to the moon back then?"

Bobby continued to stare up at the lunar landscape. It looked so peaceful up there. Was it so fantastical to think that people had once walked up there, back in the time before the Divergence? "Perhaps, I guess."

Katy sighed. "Bobby, does the moon have a name?"

"What do you mean?"

"Well, does it have a name or is it just called *the moon*?"

Something moved, back in Bobby's memory. "Dad used to tell me old, *very* old stories about times when people thought the planets were gods, creatures that influenced the lives of humans. They all had names. I think he said that some people called the moon Selene."

"Selene." The name rolled around Katy's mouth. "That's a pretty name. I like that. I think, when I'm a grown up, I'll be called Selene."

Bobby chuckled. "Don't be silly. It doesn't work like that. People don't change their names. The name we're given as a baby is the one that we keep." He turned to watch his sister as tiredness started to creep across his weary limbs. She lay there, still gazing up at the moon which cast its pale light down on her young, innocent features. He couldn't help but feel that it made her appear deathly white. Bobby shuddered. It was as if it wasn't his kid sister lying there right now, but someone else. Someone a lot older. He sighed and pushed the thoughts from his head. He had too many other things to worry about right now. "You do say silly things, sometimes."

But Katy didn't reply. She was fast asleep.

Bobby closed his eyes and joined her.

A.S.Chambers

Chapter Four

The next day, the weather was rather pleasant. As a result, Katy was in a surprisingly good mood when she awoke.

For once.

"How long do you think it'll take us to get to Orchester?" she asked as she smacked a few innocent weeds around the head with a random stick that she had discovered by the roadside that morning.

"Not long," Bobby replied, dodging around a deep rut in the road. The last thing he wanted right now was to be ankle-deep in mud. "It's only the next village along. The sun shouldn't have travelled too far across the sky. Perhaps mid-afternoon."

There was a sharp snicking sound as Katy's stick sent a yellow flower hurtling off

43

into a ditch. "Whoa!" she exclaimed. "Did you see that?"

Bobby chuckled. "Great shot, but we'd better keep the pace up if we want to make good time. I think Persephone would want us to get this talisman delivered as quick as possible."

Katy quickened her pace, catching up with her brother and leaving the offending weeds behind her. She didn't abandon her stick though. Instead, she waved it in front of her as if it were a sword. "Take that," she shouted, lunging forward with a quick jab before swiping it across an imaginary foe. "And that!"

Bobby turned and watched. "And just who are you saving the world from right now?"

"Who do you think?" Katy glowered.

Bobby frowned. "Katy, you can't let Teller get to you like this."

"But, he's horrid."

"I know, but we've left him behind in Irl-ingbury. He's of no matter to us now."

Katy harrumphed in a manner unsuited to a small girl. "I think I'd rather keep practicing, just in case," and she continued to swipe and jab at her unseen enemy.

"Careful with that. You'll have your eye out."

The two children stopped still and looked for the source of the voice.

"Who... who's there?" Bobby stammered, trying to sound a lot braver than he felt.

"Show yourself, or I'll stab you with my sword!" his little sister cried.

The voice chuckled. "But how can you stab what you cannot see, little one?"

Katy frowned. The disembodied voice had a point.

"Don't worry. I mean you no harm." There was a rustling from some overgrown hedgerow by a copse of withered trees near the roadside and a man appeared from the undergrowth. To the children, he seemed terribly old, simply by the fact that his hair was white and his skin was incredibly wrinkled. His clothing was fashioned from patches of rags and furs that had been crudely stitched together and he was hunched over, using a hefty staff to support his bent frame as he carefully eased himself up onto the road.

Bobby positioned himself between the stranger and his kid sister. The man was smiling, but that did not mean he wasn't dangerous. "You startled us."

"Well, please accept my apologies," the elderly man said. "It was not my intention." He limped closer, until he was but a short distance from the children.

Katy wrinkled her nose. "You smell," she noted.

"Katy!" Bobby hissed.

The man just laughed. "I'm sure that I do, as do most things that have not dwelt in civilisation, or what is left of it, for a good number of years. Now what are two children doing, straying far from home?"

"We are going to visit family in the next village," Bobby lied, before Katy could blurt out their real mission. There was no way that he wanted to tell anyone who they did not know what they were *really* doing.

The man closed one eye and peered at them with the other. "Are you now? Are you now?" he mused.

Bobby shifted uncomfortably under the perceptive stare and there was an awkward moment when no one said anything, not even Katy.

"Well," the stranger finally said, gripping the tip of his staff between his gnarled hands. "I'd better not keep you. Just be careful on your journey.

"You never know who you'll meet." With that, he turned to head back off the road.

"Wait a minute," Bobby called out to the old timer's hunched back. "Have you eaten today?"

The man paused, seem to consider the question, then replied, "Well, come to think of it, I don't think that I have."

Bobby reached into his tunic pocket and drew out one of the remaining apples that they had stolen from the market. He handed it over to the strange man. "My father once said that we should never see anyone go hungry, even if they were not known to us."

The man smiled as he took the apple. "Why, thank you, youngster. Your father must be a wise man. What is his name?"

"He was called Howard. He was a wood carver in Irlingbury, but he has been dead some years now."

The man stowed the apple away in a deep pocket and continued to stare at the youngsters. "A terrible thing to lose one's father, especially when so young. Tell me, how did he die?"

Bobby took a deep breath as he re-called the awful day. He and his father had been at market as usual and everything had seemed very pleasant to start with.

Until the Shadow Wraiths had descen-ded on the village.

Dressed in their obsidian robes, the servants of Kanor cantered into the village marketplace on their giant black horses and dismounted right in front of his father's stall. Riding with them was Teller and his own father. The other man whispered something to the leader of the Wraiths and then pointed down at the woodworker. Two of the Wraiths grabbed Howard and hauled him out into the town square. Bobby screamed and tried to stop them, but another Wraith grabbed him and snatched him off his feet, holding him tight. To this day he could still feel the hard, unmovable arm wrapped around his chest. It had felt more like a fired pot than human flesh. There was no give, no movement to the flesh as he strained and struggled to try and reach his father.

The woodworker called out to him, "Bobby! No! Stay there!"

The leader of the Wraiths lowered his black hood, revealing a face that was truly unforgettable: skin impossibly smooth, as if fashioned from glass, and hair slicked close against his scalp. "This is what happens to traitors!" he declared to the startled villagers that had been shopping for their goods as he held his hand out in front of Bobby's father. In a quick stabbing motion, the hand transformed into a long, stake-like weapon and plunged deep into the man's chest.

Howard was dead before he hit the floor.

As Bobby screamed and cried, the commander of the Wraiths just peered across at him with a curious look in his eyes.

Then the Shadow Wraiths simply

climbed back up on their horses and rode out of town, leaving Bobby and Katy behind: orphans.

"He... he was executed by the Shadow Wraiths," Bobby summarised. Not wanting to relive the details any more than he had to. "They said he was a traitor, but he was just a woodworker. He had never done anything wrong."

Bobby turned at the sound of a wet sniff from his kid sister. He shook his head and held out his arms. She threw herself into his side and buried her face into his clothing. He felt his own tears start to burn at the sides of his eyes.

The old stranger sighed. "Many evil things have been done in the name of the law, child. Perhaps, one day, the law will change."

Bobby nodded, forcing back the tears. He did not want to cry, not in front of this strange man, not in front of Katy.

The man lay a disfigured hand on the teenager's shoulder. It felt incredibly heavy, far heavier than one would have expected. "I wish you well, Bobby. Walk well and stay safe."

"Thank you, sir," the boy replied. "Tell me, what is your name?"

"The name I use is Cutter, and I hope that we meet again." With that, he turned and vanished once more into the under-growth.

Bobby sighed and turned to his kid sister. "Come on," he said. "Let's get going."

As the two children carried on along the bumpy road, Katy asked her brother. "Bobby, how did that man know your name?"

A.S.Chambers

Chapter Five

Bobby was deep in thought as he and Katy trudged along the ill-maintained road to Orchester. The encounter with the man called Cutter had left him deeply unsettled.

First, there was the memory of his father's death at the hand of the Shadow Wraiths. The boy could not get his final image of his father out of his head as he called out Bobby's name. That alone was enough to tie his stomach in knots.

Then there was the mysterious Cutter. How had the old man known his name? Bobby kept going over the conversation in his head to see if he had forgotten something. Perhaps Katy had said his name? Perhaps he had introduced himself and had forgotten?

"Perhaps he already knew us?" Katy suggested, stepping carefully between rank, festering puddles.

Bobby considered this. It was possible. The old man could have met them before.

But surely he would have remembered him?

The older sibling shook his head with a fair amount of hesitation. "I don't know, Katy. I didn't recognise him at all, and I think he has a face that we would remember." He thrust his hands in his pockets and his fingers latched onto the small wooden talisman. He rubbed his thumb over the engraved surface and felt the distinct shapes of the sword and the cup. He needed to keep a clear head if he was to fulfil his promise to Persephone.

It was then that he heard the sound of horses' hooves pounding up the road behind them.

"Katy! Quick! Hide!"

Bobby grabbed his sister's arm and pulled her off the side of the road into the brush and thicket that grew in the parallel ditch. For once, she didn't protest. She could hear the alarm in his voice. Their feet squelched in the filth and the mire and Bobby felt the ground give way beneath him, causing him to slide unceremoniously down into a stagnant pool of scum-covered water. As he was holding onto Katy, he could not help but drag her down with him but, to give his sister her dues, she didn't shout out in surprise.

They righted themselves and hunkered down in the dirt and the weeds, pulling the undergrowth around them to keep them shielded from unwelcome eyes, but allowing enough space to see who was riding along the otherwise empty road.

As the two children crouched down in the thick, unwelcoming undergrowth, Bobby curled his arm around his kid sister desperate to protect her from the one thing that the sound of horse beats could mean: trouble. He kept his breathing shallow as four horses cantered to a halt right in front of them. Someone dismounted and Bobby peered through the scratty undergrowth to see who it was. Nausea rose in his gut as he immediately recognised the rider.

It was Teller.

"What do you see?" came a voice from one of the other riders. Bobby couldn't make out who it was, but he was guessing that it was one of the bully's cronies.

"I'm not sure," Teller replied, bending down to peer into the dirt where Bobby and Katy had been walking just a short moment ago.

Bobby's blood ran cold as his hand instinctively slipped into his pocket.

His *empty* pocket!

Oh no! This was definitely not good.

Teller stood up, dusting off his discovery. "Look at this," he instructed his companions. "What do you make of it?" The four riders peered down at the talisman. "You think that's a sword and some sort of cup?"

"You think it's Normal's?"

"I doubt anyone else has been along here."

"What do you think he was doing with it?" one of the others asked.

"Not got a clue, but my bet is that traitorous little piece of pigswill was up to no good."

Teller pocketed the artefact and re-mounted his steed. "Come on, there's a field up ahead where we can camp and rest for a bit. They're on foot. We'll soon catch them up, so there's no immediate hurry."

And, with that, the four rode off in possession of the one thing that Bobby had sworn to keep safe.

Once he was sure that Teller and his gang were at a distance from where he could not be seen, Bobby clambered up out of the ditch. His garments were muddy and his hands were cut. What was worse, his heart was weighted down as if with a handful of lead. He had failed. Persephone had trusted him and he had failed.

He felt a small hand slip into his and he looked down at Katy. "What are we to do?" he asked.

"Simple," she replied. "We need to get it back."

True to their word, Teller and his companions camped in the field that they had mentioned. They tied their horses to an old tree and set a campfire close by. For fuel, they burnt hunks of decayed wood that they had scavenged from the remains of a rotten tree after igniting some scrubby bits of dried bracken for kindling. The remains of an overgrown hedge traced the perimeter of the enclosure and it was through this that Bobby and Katy spied on the thieves, working out what they should do to recover the precious talisman.

"What's the plan?" the younger sibling asked the older.

Bobby thought about it for a moment. "Well, we can't just walk in and take it, can we? We'll have to wait until they go to sleep and grab it then."

"How will we see? It'll be pitch black!"

Bobby shook his head. "No, it won't. Think about the moon last night. It was full. Once it rises, we should have enough light to let us find the talisman whilst it being dark enough to conceal us in the shadows."

Katy nodded and they continued to observe the four riders who seemed to be deep in conversation. Bobby watched them hand the talisman around and turn it over, studying it, trying to discern its purpose. In the end, they apparently gave up and Teller stashed the wooden artefact in his saddle-bag which lay next to him on the grass by the fire. He pulled a bottle out of the same saddlebag and there was the sound of cheers from his companions as he un-stoppered the cork and took a long, thirsty swig before passing it around.

Eventually, the sky turned dark as the stars and the moon rose above. Teller and his companions started to stretch and yawn. Bobby watched anxiously as they unrolled their beds and settled down to sleep. Within minutes, the sound of drunken snoring reached the ears of the children.

Bobby pried his way through the hedgerow. "Come on. Now's our chance." Carefully, he tiptoed his way into the make-shift camp. The only sounds that he could hear were the loud snoring, the crackling of the fire and the pounding drumbeat of his heart. If Teller or one of his companions were to wake...

Bobby shoved that thought out of his head. He had to concentrate on retrieving the talisman. He could not let it stay in the possession of this cruel thug.

Easing himself around the fire, he approached the sleeping Teller. The older boy was flat on his back with his mouth wide open. Bobby winced at the rank breath that came from the bully's mouth. Then he paled when he realised where the saddlebag was. Teller was using it as a pillow!

This was not good. How on earth was he supposed to reach into the bag's pocket and grab the talisman? Quietly, he crouched down onto his haunches and looked closely at the bag. It was well and truly lodged under his enemy's head and there was no way of reaching into it.

Just as he was considering this dilemma there was a noise. The horses gave a brusque snort and stamped their feet. Teller's mouth closed and reopened as vague words were mumbled through his sleepy lips. Bobby felt as if he were going to be sick. If the older boy woke up right now, he would be done for! Instead, Teller grimaced, drew his blanket up tight and rolled over to his left. As he did so, his head rolled off the pocket of the saddlebag.

Bobby seized the opportunity. He darted forwards and quickly unclasped the buckle. Before the older boy could roll back, his hand snaked inside the depths of the leather bag, rooted around and found something small and hard. His face grinned in the moonlight as he snatched the talisman out and stashed it back into his pocket.

He was just about to move away into the night when an almighty crash came from behind him. His head snapped back to see Katy flat on her face with a piece of food in her hand. By the looks of her, she had been following the demands of her stomach and had been rifling through a promising saddlebag before promptly tripping over its treacherous long straps.

Bobby winced then blanched as he turned back to be confronted with the furious face of the now wide-awake Teller. The last thing he saw before a painful blackness grabbed him was the older boy's fist hammering towards his face.

A.S.Chambers

Chapter Six

"Bobby! Bobby!"

Bobby had been dreaming. He wasn't sure what he had been dreaming *about*, but he realised that he didn't like it much. It was mostly shadows and silhouettes, as if the subjects of the dream were standing in front of a very bright light. There was a cup, a sword and something his mind would not let him recognise. Something with large black wings. This last thing filled him with a terrible fear that twisted the very base of his stomach.

Its mouth was moving, but Bobby was unable to hear any discernible words. It was as if the voice of the creature was coming from a long, long way away; as if the sounds were travelling from a place either far in the past or the future. There was just the *feeling* of words, a three-pulse pattern repeating over and over like an erratic triple time beat of a heart.

"Bobby! Bobby!"

The creature had lurched closer now and the light behind it was blindingly bright. Bobby could make out gnarled claws at the end of its powerful black arms. As the light streamed between the outstretched talons, they opened and shut in hungry, grasping motions, reaching out desperately for the cup and the sword that remained tantalisingly out of its avaricious reach.

"Bobby! Bobby!"

It was closer still. There was a smell from the creature that made Bobby want to roll over and vomit the contents of his gut onto the floor. It was rank and sulphurous. It was the odour of a thing that shouldn't be, that was completely unnatural. The threefold sound increased in pitch and volume, screaming through his tortured ears. It was dry and sibilant, passionate and desperate.

He strained as best as he could to make out the words that were sliding from the gaping maw of the monster that so desperately wanted the cup and the sword. He screamed out into the dream that he wanted to hear what was being said, that he *needed* to hear what was being said.

"We... are... one!" came the cruel voice. "We... are... one!"

And the monster was upon him, its head to his. Bobby continued to scream into the nightmare as all the world around him began to dissolve away. He looked left and right, seeing fields and villages put to the torch. Armies of constructs marched across the barren land, slaying all who stood before them.

"Bobby! Bobby!"

"We... are... one!" the voice insisted once more, before the beast opened an obsidian eyelid and its snake-like eye peered deep into Bobby's heart, judging whether or not he should be consumed like the rest of the world.

"Bobby! Wake up!"

Another voice, closer this time. Right next to him, in fact. The boy opened his eyes and immediately regretted the move as pain erupted down the side of his head. "Ow," he murmured.

"Bobby? You okay?"

Bobby Normal groaned as he inched his head up into a position to look at his sister. She was sat on the ground next to him, concern on her face. He tried to reach out to her but discovered that his hands were tied firmly behind his back.

Then he remembered Teller and groaned again.

"I'm okay," he managed to say. "You?"

Katy nodded.

"Well, well, well," came a mocking voice. "The food thief is awake at last. What happened, Normal? Take a little tumble?" Teller's cronies cackled in response to the pathetic joke. However, it made Bobby realise something and he tried to rub his leg against the inside of his trousers. He felt something small and hard inside the fabric. Yes! The talisman was still there. The idiots had assumed that they had just been raiding the camp for food, so hadn't bothered to search him.

Now, if only they could escape...

However, escape was far from Teller's plans. "Well lads, I think we need to make an example of these two. Make sure that they remember that thieving is a crime."

The teenager's cronies chuckled darkly as Teller unfurled his prize possession, his vicious whip. He made a great show of stretching it out and flexing it this way and that. In the still dark, the sound of the creaking leather was all that could be heard.

Then there were three sharp cracks as he flicked it left, right, left, grinning cruelly as he did. It was intended as a demonstration of his mastery of the weapon, to show that *he* was the one in complete control here.

Bobby didn't move a muscle. In his head he recalled the images from his dream: the large dark creature that hungered ravenously for the cup and the sword. He remembered the feelings of pure terror that it had brewed inside of him. That was something to *truly* fear, not some bratty teenage upstart with a whip and an inflated ego.

Teller frowned at the lack of response from his captive. "Playing the hero, Normal?" he sneered, coiling up his whip. "You think you're just going to walk away from this? Think you're better than us? Than me? That's what your father thought and look where it got him." He flicked his whip out and a sharp snapping sound echoed first through Bobby's left ear, then his right. "You are nothing, Normal! Nothing, I say!"

Again, Teller cracked the whip either side of Bobby's head.

Still Bobby did not flinch. This was nothing to fear. The creature in the dream was *something* to fear. He saw it reaching out, grasping for the cup and the sword. The cup and the sword that were engraved onto the surface of the Eternal Talisman. As Teller ranted and raved unimportant words in front of him, Bobby withdrew inside. The nightmare and the talisman must be linked; the imagery was the same. But what was the creature? Why did it want the cup and the sword? What were they to it?

Bobby's left cheek stung as the whip nicked the skin just below his eye.

Still he did not respond. His mind was still concentrating on deeper, more important things. The creature had been speaking in the dream. "We are one," it had said, over and over. What did that mean? It had to be important. If he could figure that out…

It was then that three other words snapped Bobby back to the here and now.

"Bring the girl."

Katy kicked and bit as two of the thugs dragged her over to their grinning leader.

Bobby tried to lunge forward to save his kid sister. However, the other goon kept a firm hand on his shoulder to prevent him from interfering as Teller drew out a huge hunting knife that glinted wickedly in the un-natural white light of the full moon.

"Aha!" Teller crowed with delight. "At last we have our guest's attention. Fun at last!"

Katy fell terribly silent while he ran the flat of the blade across her smooth cheek. "What do you think, lads? A nice big cross to show the world just what a horrid piece of work she is? That okay, Normal? Every time you look at it, you can remember just how insolent you were to me."

Bobby struggled to break free but only

managed to receive a sharp blow to the head for his troubles. All he could do was watch helplessly as Katy wept in fear, the wicked point of the blade approaching her face.

It was then that they all heard the long, mournful howl from out in the dark.

Teller froze, the knife still poised a breath away from the girl's cheek. Bobby watched as the bully's eyes widened and scanned the perimeter of the camp. "What the hell was that?" he snapped. "Find out what it was!" he barked at the other older boys.

The three exchanged glances, obviously not wanting to be the first to wander off into the surrounding night.

"Now!" Teller yelled, waving the hunting knife in their direction.

As a trio, they edged towards the point on the perimeter of the camp from where they thought the noise had originated. Then there was a stomach-churning roar and something large and hairy flew through the air, flattening two of the hoodlums. The third gave off a falsetto shriek and ran back towards the fire.

Bobby turned as best as he could to watch the beast. It paced slowly forwards on all fours, its grey hair bristling in the flickering light of the fire, malice in its dark eyes as it stalked towards Teller who was waving his knife towards it. A knife that, in Bobby's opinion, now seemed incredibly ineffective.

Then something miraculous happened.

The beast spoke.

"You harm so much as a hair on that young girl's head and I will make you watch whilst I slowly devour your pathetic entrails." It padded further into the camp, it's head low and menacing. It was now so close that Bobby could actually feel the heat from its immense, muscular body. "You will get on your horses and leave this place. Now!"

Teller and his companions did not need instructing twice. They launched up onto their horses and galloped off into the night, not once looking back.

The beast sat down on its haunches and gave what seemed to be an amused grunt of satisfaction. It turned its head to face Bobby, who was desperately trying to wrench the bonds from his wrists. He had no desire for him and Katy to be this creature's supper. Then he stopped as the animal seemed to laugh.

"They may have been cowards but they seem to have tied rather good knots. Wouldn't you say so, Bobby?" Then, right in front of the boy's amazed eyes, the beast's features seemed to melt and transform until there on the ground sat the old man from before, Cutter.

Chapter Seven

A short while later, Bobby and Katy were devouring a simple broth that Cutter had produced from some of the provisions that Teller's party had left behind as they had fled for their pitiful lives. As he spooned the tasty meal into his mouth, Bobby kept glancing over the top of the bowl at their saviour. Rather than joining in with the food, the old man was sat quietly, drawing deeply on a long, hand-fashioned pipe, its fragrant smoke drifting up into the night-time air.

When he had finished his food, Bobby lay his bowl down next to him and spoke. "Thank you."

"It was the best that I could do with what those cowards left behind," Cutter shrugged.

"That's not what I meant. You saved our lives."

The old man shrugged again.

Bobby continued to stare at him, the moonlight making his face appear pale, mystical.

"What are you?"

"I am an old man."

"I've never met an old man who can turn into a wolf."

"So, I'm a *special* old man," Cutter smiled as he blew a smoke ring into the air.

Bobby's eyes never left him.

Katy produced a small, ripe belch as she finished her food. "Does it hurt?" she asked.

Cutter raised an eyebrow for her to explain.

"When you change like that. Does it hurt?"

The old man shook his head. "No. There is no pain."

"But surely all your bones get bent and twisted? That must hurt a lot."

Cutter chuckled as he tapped his pipe in the palm of his hand in thought. "How much do you know of long ago. In the time before the Divergence?"

"Not much," Bobby admitted. "Dad used to tell us bits and pieces, but they were only fragments." He noticed a certain sadness cross the old man's face.

"Did your father ever tell you about the Bloodline of Abel?" Cutter asked, the sadness quickly dissipating, a harder look forming on his face.

Both children shook their heads.

The man took a long draw from his pipe and continued. "They were a group of people with special abilities that enabled them to become wolves. They were powerful, strong. But they were also greedy. They thought only of themselves."

Katy frowned. "But you're not greedy. You just saved us and fed us."

"I am not of the Bloodline," Cutter shrugged, "but those morons before did not know that. No, the Bloodline died out many, many years ago. Before the Divergence. Before Kanor."

"How did they die out, if they were so strong?" Katy asked.

The fire cracked and spat up into the air.

Cutter watched a mote of singed wood spiral up into the night.

"They crossed the wrong man," he growled.

"Then who are you?" Bobby asked.

Cutter watched the fire dance in the dark. "Just an old man who has made too many mistakes. But right now," he smiled as Katy let out a huge yawn, "I believe that you two should be getting some sleep."

The next morning, Bobby awoke with a stiff crick in his neck but, aside from that, he felt relatively refreshed.

There had been no nightmares.

As he lay on his back, gently rocking his head from side to side in an attempt to loosen his protesting muscles, he gazed up at the lightening sky and watched fluffy clouds drift across the wide blue above him.

Had the skies been the same before the Divergence? he wondered to himself. He knew that the land had changed dramatically when Kanor had risen and unleashed his merciless constructs. Before, there had been huge cities and machines with people travelling up and down the country as well as up into the skies beyond the planet. Now there was barren countryside and the occasional ramshackle village. The Divergence had changed the very ground upon which people walked.

But had it changed the skies?

Before the decimation of the human race, had people been able to lie back like he was doing right now and look up at clouds dancing lazily in exactly the same manner?

Bobby did not know. There was so much that he did not know of the time before the Divergence. Cutter's tale last night of men being able to turn into wolves had whetted his appetite. What else had there been?

Speaking of Cutter.

Bobby sat up and looked around for the curious old man, but he was nowhere to be seen. There was just Katy, snoring loudly under her grey blanket.

What was the old man? People could

not change shape like that. He claimed to not be of the Bloodline, but surely he had to be something else. Something special. Also, was he following them? First, he had appeared out of apparently nowhere on the roadside, then he miraculously turned up last night to save them. Then Bobby recalled a memory from when they had left Irlingbury. Teller had called out to his companions that he had seen Bobby down the street. They had gone running off in the opposite direction. Who had they seen? If Cutter could change shape…

Then there was that nightmare, the creature that wanted the cup and the sword that were on the Eternal Talisman. Bobby slipped the artefact out of his pocket and traced the engraving with his thumb. What did it stand for? Were they actual things? Were they weapons to help this Virtuous Man defeat Kanor?

So many questions for so early in the day.

Bobby shrugged as his stomach rumbled. It was time to eat and time to wake his kid sister.

She would only be pleased at one of those two facts.

"So, how far is Orchester?"

Bobby sighed. "Like I said just yesterday, not far?"

"I know. But *how* far?"

"We should be there soon."

"But how long is *soon*?"

Bobby took a deep, steadying breath. The petulant questions had been non-stop since Katy had finished filling her mouth with breakfast. "I should think, by the time that the sun is at the top of the sky."

Katy peered up into the blue sky. "That's *ages*."

"No, it's not."

"Is. My feet hurt."

Bobby groaned and turned to face his whining sibling, but when he looked into her brown eyes he saw that she was telling the truth. Her mouth was turned down, her shoulders sloped and her face sad. "How bad?" he asked.

"Lots."

He studied his sister's feet - clad in a

pitifully cheap pair of home-made leather boots that they had scavenged a few weeks back. The thinning material was scuffed and torn, her small toes poking through.

Bobby sighed as the guilt of dragging his sister along washed over him. "Let's take a break," he suggested.

"I want to go home," Katy whispered.

"We can't. We have to deliver the talisman, remember?"

Katy flumped down onto the side of the track, dust pluming up around her. "I don't care about the stupid talisman. I don't care about Orchester. My feet hurt. I'm hungry. I want to go to sleep in a comfy bed. I don't want mean boys trying to hurt me..." She trailed off as the tears came.

Bobby felt his heart crumble and, seating himself next to his kid sister, he wrapped her in his arms. "I'm sorry," he apologised, his voice brimming over with remorse, "I truly am. But people are depending on us."

"But why us?" she sobbed into his shoulder.

The image of the beast in the nightmare slunk back into his head.

"Because there is no one else," Bobby replied.

He pushed the dark creature away and instead let his mind drift back to some years previous. A happier time when there had been three of them. He thought about playing with Katy and their dad in the fields on a long hot summer's day.

"Do you remember playing *horse* with Dad?"

Bobby felt his sister's head rub against his shoulder.

"I've got an idea."

Sometime later, Bobby's feet were red raw, his back ached and he was fit to drop, but his heart was soaring to the sound of Katy giggling and laughing up on his back. It had been incredibly awkward helping her up there (he wasn't as tall as their father and she was all elbows and knees), but once he had worked out the intricate balancing act, he had found himself quite adept at dodging the ruts and potholes in the road to the neighbouring village.

As the sun reached the pinnacle of its

daytime journey, the children started to once again observe signs of habitation and they galloped into their destination: the village of Orchester.

Chapter Eight

Bobby hadn't really known what to expect from Orchester. All he had ever known, as far as villages were concerned, was Irlingbury. He had been born there, grown up there and, like the majority of its residents, had never ever left its not too sizeable boundary.

He had to admit that, as they walked into the neighbouring settlement, he was somewhat disappointed. It looked identical to his home village. The streets were muddy and rutted, the houses patched together with whatever random materials the townsfolk could scavenge and the inhabitants wore the same look of tired despair as did those from just a few miles down the road.

"Looks like home," Katy observed.

Bobby nodded. "I know."

"So, where have we got to go?"

Bobby's forehead creased as he re-called Persephone's instructions. "We're looking for a man called Jason. She said that he would be in a small house on the main road entering the village and that there would be a green mark on the door. Some sort of face."

"A happy one or a sad one?"

Bobby shrugged at the random question of an eight-year-old. "I have absolutely no idea. Let's go and find out. It shouldn't take too long, we're already on the main road."

The two children walked slowly down the centre of the street, their eyes scanning each door as they passed them by. Like in Irlingbury, they were all made from wood and each one was shut, unwelcoming, bar-ring out any passing horrors or servants of Kanor.

As they reached the end of the road, where it opened out into the bedraggled market square, Bobby was aware of two things.

The first was that they had not found the door with the green face. They had studied every single door that they had passed, both on the left hand side and on the right. All had been distinctly faceless.

The second was that he had a strong feeling that they were being followed. He turned and peered down the high street. It was a straight passage out of the village and there was nowhere to hide, yet he was sure that there was someone there, lurking in the shadows. When he had been younger, his father had once taken him hunting for rabbits. They had found what his father had considered a suitable spot and had set up three snares, then retired behind the crest of a small mound and waited. In time, a diminutive rabbit had hopped out into the open and had started to sniff around, its tiny nose flicking its long whiskers this way and that. Bobby had felt his father's large hand come to rest on his shoulder. Peering up, he had seen the tall man place two fingers to his lips – an order for total silence. Yet, even with this silence, the rabbit had paused in what it was doing. It had stood up on its hind legs and peered around and about. Then without any warning, it had turned tail and scarpered. Bobby had asked his father to explain how the rabbit had known they were there, even though they hadn't made a sound. His father had mulled this over for a moment then had said, "Sometimes, it doesn't matter just how careful you are, just how many precautions you take, the little critter that you're following will simply, intuitively *know*. Something deep down inside of it will start tingling and ringing out like bells used to hundreds of years ago. It will sense this alarm and know that, right now, it ought to be somewhere else sharpish."

Right now, Bobby felt just like that little rabbit. He couldn't explain it, but he just knew, deep down, that he and Katy were not alone.

And this made him incredibly uneasy.

He was about to take Katy by the hand and lead her back down the street on another attempt at locating the green face whilst keeping an eye open for anyone who might be following them, when he realised that she wasn't there. His head snapped this way and that as his heart began to thump in his chest and his panic rose. All around were villagers going about their usual routine, milling around the few stalls that occupied the market square. They were bartering and haggling with stall vendors, oblivious to a worried teenage boy having lost his kid sister.

Bobby took a step towards the crowd of people, desperate to try and spot Katy in their midst, but all he could see was a mass of browns and greys of ragged homemade clothing identical to that which he and Katy wore. He ran his fingers through his brown hair and bit down on his lower lip. Tears were starting to well in the corners of his eyes.

Had someone snatched Katy away from him when he wasn't looking?

Why had he agreed to come here?

Why had he agreed to bring the talisman to a man he didn't even know?

He had put his and Katy's life in danger and now he was going to have to pay the price.

He heard the familiar crunch of a purloined apple, followed by, "What's the matter?"

Bobby stared down at the grubby little face that was merrily munching away on a freshly acquired piece of fruit. "Katy! Where have you been?"

"Getting food. Want an apple?" She offered one up to him.

Bobby saw red. "I have been worried sick! Don't you dare run off like that! Anything could have happened to you."

His kid sister swallowed and paused her munching. "But… I was only over there. I could see you."

"But *I* couldn't see *you*."

The eight-year-old harrumphed and crossed her arms. "I'm perfectly capable of taking care of myself," she grumbled.

No explanation, however, was going to stop her older brother. The stress and the strain of the last couple of days welled up inside of him and began to overflow. "No. No you can't. You're too young. You're my responsibility. I have to look after you. You're all I've got left!"

"I am *not* too young," Katy stormed as

she stamped her foot. "I am perfectly capable of looking after myself. I got these, didn't I?" She thrust the apples up in her brother's face.

"But that's just apples. What if there was something more serious? More dangerous?"

"I'd work something out."

"Oh, really? You'd be able to take on a construct? Perhaps a Shadow Wraith or even one of the Fallen?"

"Yes, I would!"

"No, you wouldn't. They were the ones who killed Dad, remember? If he couldn't escape them, then neither of us stand a chance."

And then he realised that, in letting his deepest fears spill out from his mouth, he had overstepped the mark.

Katy's lip began to tremble and tears welled up in her brown eyes. "You know I don't like it when you talk about how Dad died."

Bobby ran his fingers through his hair. "Oh, Katy, I'm sorry. I just…" He reached out to hold the sobbing girl, but she pushed him

away and darted off into the crowd of shop-
pers.

The boy swore under his breath and
ploughed in after her.

It was like pushing his way through a
vertical sea of mud. Numerous market-go-
ers and vendors shouted abuse and yelled
insults at the apparently rude teenage boy
who shoved at them and heaved them away
as he desperately tried to keep sight of his
kid sister. She, being smaller, was having a
far easier time of dodging around the irate
villagers of Orchester. Katy nipped under
their arms and darted between their legs as
she kept a consistent distance and pace
ahead of her pursuing brother.

When they reached the opposite edge
of the market square, the throng of people
started to thin out and Katy made a break for
a wide road that was situated on the far side.
She glanced over her shoulder and hurtled
along the broken, uneven road surface,
heading for a stone bridge that rose up in
front of her.

She never saw Teller step out of the

dark side alley.

She couldn't even scream as he wrapped his arm around her mouth and dragged her up onto the bridge.

"Don't come any closer!" the older boy shouted down to Bobby, who had finally managed to extricate himself from the crowd. "Remember, I have a knife!"

Bobby skidded to a halt as Teller drew the familiar weapon from its scabbard. The sunlight glinted on its highly polished surface as the thug pressed it close to Katy's neck. The frantic brother held his hands out in front of him in a pacifying manner. "Okay, okay! I see it. I see it. Now, what's going on?"

Teller continued to back up onto the bridge, Katy clasped awkwardly in his arm. "I want to make you suffer, Normal, that's what. I want it so that every time you look at your brat of a sister, you'll know that I won."

Bobby shook his head. "What... what on earth do you mean? Won? Won what? This isn't a game!"

"But it is to you, isn't it? It's all a game. You flaunt the rules. You beg, you steal. You consort with those who would overthrow the power that rules us."

Bobby blanched. Instinctively, his hand darted into his pocket and felt the Eternal Talisman safely tucked away. Teller hadn't mentioned it before. Yes, he had found it on the road to here, but he had had no idea as to what it was or what Persephone had asked him to do.

He had to be talking about something else.

"What do you mean?"

The older boy let out a bray of laughter and tightened the wicked knife up against Katy's neck. "You seriously expect me to believe you have no idea what your father was up to?"

"My f… father," Bobby stammered, "was a woodworker."

"Your *f…father*," Teller mocked, "was a dissident. He plotted against those above us. He planned to overthrow Kanor himself!"

Bobby's mouth hung open. It wasn't true. It couldn't be true. How on earth could there be any truth to this?

Teller chuckled to himself then grinned

maniacally as he raised the knife to Katy's grubby cheek.

His laughter was cut short in a scream of pain as the young girl bit down onto his other hand. He drew back in shock, waving his bleeding hand in front of him. Katy advanced and shoved him as hard as she could in his midriff. Normally, due to her comparative lack of size and weight, this would have been a completely ineffectual move, but two things played to her advantage. First, Teller was already off-balance, his concentration centred more on the bleeding hand than the enraged eight-year-old girl. Second, as he had backed up along the bridge, he had inadvertently edged closer and closer to the low parapet. As he flailed his arm around in pain, the minimal force of Katy's hands caused him to stumble and catch his hip against the crumbling stonework which immediately broke and gave way beneath him.

Teller tumbled over the side.

Bobby charged up to the crest of the bridge and joined his sister at the point where the older boy had fallen. They looked down and saw no flowing river but a dried-up bed of mud and stone. Across one of the larger boulders lay the broken body of Teller, his neck at a most unnatural angle.

"I told you that I could look after my-self," Katy whispered.

Bobby turned to his sister, a look of horror on his face.

She, in turn, peered along the road that led past the bridge. "Look," she said, "this road leads out the other end of town. Come on. That house we're looking for might be along here."

It didn't take the two children long to find the door with the small painting of a wild-looking green face painted towards its top. Bobby, however, wasn't exactly con-centrating on the task at hand.

His kid sister had just killed someone and was showing no remorse whatsoever.

How? Just how could this be?

Was it Katy? Was she some sort of hardened killer now? No, he refused to be-lieve that.

Was it shock? That seemed more

likely. Perhaps her mind was shutting down any reaction to what she had done, concentrating on another task to protect her.

Was it something bigger? Was it the world in which they were growing up? Had they grown up in a different time, they would have lived as children, been loved by their parents and been able to spend their time playing games. Here, however, they were on their own. A cruel monster ruled the world and they were considered the lowest of the low. Death was an everyday occurrence in this world. Was the atmosphere in which they lived fashioning them? Would *he* be the same as Katy was right now, should he have to kill someone to survive?

He did not know which of these was the correct answer.

"Well?" his kid sister asked as she stood before the door. "Are you going to knock?"

Bobby snapped back to the task at hand and nodded. He lifted his right hand to the wood and rapped three times with his knuckles. There was a short wait and they could hear the sound of movement behind the door. Then a high-pitched, reverberating squeal came from the creaking, unoiled hinges as the door swung inwards and the face of an elderly woman peered around its edge. "Yes?" she asked.

Bobby took a deep breath and re-peated what Persephone had told him. "We have come to deliver the goods."

Immediately, the woman's face seemed to become twenty years younger. Her mouth rose in a beautiful smile and de-light twinkled in her grey eyes. "Oh, bless you! Bless you. You seek Jason."

Bobby nodded. "Persephone sent us."

The woman glanced up and down the street.

"Then you had better come in and I will take you to meet the Virtuous Man."

Bobby Normal will return in
Bobby Normal and the Virtuous Man.

A.S.Chambers

Author's Notes

Thank you for reading what, quite frankly, has been somewhat of a labour of love for me. The idea of writing *Bobby Normal and the Eternal Talisman* first came to me when I was writing *Sam Spallucci: Dark Justice*. There is a scene in that book where Sam first encounters a construct in the "flesh" and it really is quite chilling; the notion of this unstoppable creature of clay with no sense of love or ethics, just a golem made to hunt and kill. As I was writing that scene, I thought to myself: *What would this monster look like to a child?* So, I immediately sat down and rewrote it from the perspective of a teenage boy. In that moment, Bobby Normal was born.

I then started to ponder what else it

would be interesting to see through eyes younger than that of my normal characters and I started to think about what life would be like in a world with not just one or two constructs lumbering around the place, but whole armies of them. This was what led me to set *Eternal Talisman*, and all the books which are to follow, after the events of the Divergence. So far, we have observed glimpses of this Earth devastated by Kanor, through dreams, prophecies and vague references, but we've not had something substantial or tangible. I've known since I was a teenager, what the Divergent Lands are going to be like and, quite frankly, I've been chomping at the bit to write about them, so the Bobby Normal books will give me the chance to share more of this tortured earth as the Sam Spallucci storyline picks up speed and heads towards the act of one man who will change existence for all creation.

One thing which I felt had to change for the Bobby Normal books was the style of writing. With Sam's stories, they are all first person and very much a modern noir style with the feeling of an adult who is becoming jaded with a world that hasn't really turned out how he expected it to. It was quite apparent that this style would not work for books with children as their main characters. Yes, they have already been through a lot in their short lives, especially with the death of their parents, but there is still a feeling that there could be hope that things might change. For Bobby, there is the notion of doing something positive, whether it be helping to fight Kanor or protecting his kid sister. For Katy… well, I don't want to give too much away there just yet. Spoilers, so to speak, but there are certain clues in the book as to what fate has in store for the feisty eight-year-old. I'd be intrigued to know if you picked up on them.

So, one of the reasons why such a short book has taken so long to write (almost five years!) was that, at first, I really struggled with the style. I initially wanted it to have the feel of a Young Adult book. I wanted it to appeal to a younger audience and use it as a way to introduce new readers into the Spalluciverse. However, there was a problem: I have a personal dislike for YA fiction. Most of the books I have read in that genre really don't rock my boat, so to speak. I've found the plots over-simplistic and the characters rather cut and paste duplicates of each other. Those who know me in person know that there is a rather large franchise that I regularly have a rant about when I'm asked about publishing, but I will steer well away from that as Author's Notes are not supposed to take ten hours to read…

So it was that poor old Bobby struggled to take shape for such a long time and was pushed to one side not only by three Sam Spallucci works (*Dark Justice, Belligerent Bard* and *Troubled Souls*) but also one novella (*Songbird*), an anthology (*Mourning Has Broken*) and an omnibus (*Children of Cain*). The story was written and escapades were told, but it just did not feel *right* to me. Then, during the first Lockdown of 2020, I dipped into my vast collection of pre-Disney *Star Wars* books and started reading the *Jedi Apprentice* series by Jude Watson as my bedtime reading. The books are short, centred around characters that I love (Qui-

Gon Jinn and Obi-Wan Kenobi) and had me gripped. Aimed at a young audience, they came out after *The Phantom Menace*, serving as prequels to the prequel, telling the story of Obi-Wan's early years as a padawan learner. They became my biggest influence in writing *Eternal Talisman*. This was because they showed me it was okay to put my characters in true peril and, not only that but also that the children in the stories could perform dark deeds. Once I saw how Watson wove this into her stories, I went for it. I sat down and wrote the "tunnel scene" and enjoyed the first draft, so rewrote it and enjoyed it even more. I then sat back and had a good long look at Katy. I thought about what was going to happen to her in future books here and in the *Divergent Lands* trilogy and I knew that I had to start sowing seeds for that right now. As a result, Teller had to meet a gruesome end at the hand of an eight-year-old who would then show no remorse.

So, I highly recommend Jude Watson's books. Her old *Star Wars* ones are still out there on the Internet, but you may have to pay a premium price as they are highly collectible.

Anyway, like I said earlier, Author's Notes are not supposed to take ten hours to read, so I had better draw this to a close. At the time of writing, I have about five Bobby Normal books planned. Number two is obviously concerned with the Virtuous Man. One will be centred around the mysterious shape-changing Cutter. There will be one featuring the Children of Cain and another that features the characters who were vaguely mentioned in a throw away comment as the Fallen. As for anything else...? Well, I'm not too sure yet. I have ideas, but something wicked and cowled that way lies. We shall just have to wait and see.

ASC January 2021.

ABOUT THE AUTHOR

A.S.Chambers resides in Lancaster, England. He lives a fairly simple life measuring the growing rates of radishes and occasionally puts pen to paper to stop the voices in his head from constantly berating him.

He is quite happy for, and in fact would encourage, you to follow him on Facebook, Instagram and Twitter.

There is also a nice, shiny website:
www.aschambers.co.uk

Printed in Great Britain
by Amazon